Señor Roscoe

On Vacation

Jim Field

At the very top of a very tall building lives
a friendly dog called señor Roscoe.

¡Buenos días, señor Roscoe!

¡Buenos días!
Hello!

¡Hola!
Hi!

¿Cómo está?
How are you?

Café

Today is a special day. Señor Roscoe and his goldfish, Fry, are going on vacation to visit their friends.
Hola, me llamo señor Roscoe.
Hello, my name is Mr. Roscoe.
Vacations

It's time to pack. There are lots of things to remember.

Don't forget your toothbrush, señor Roscoe!

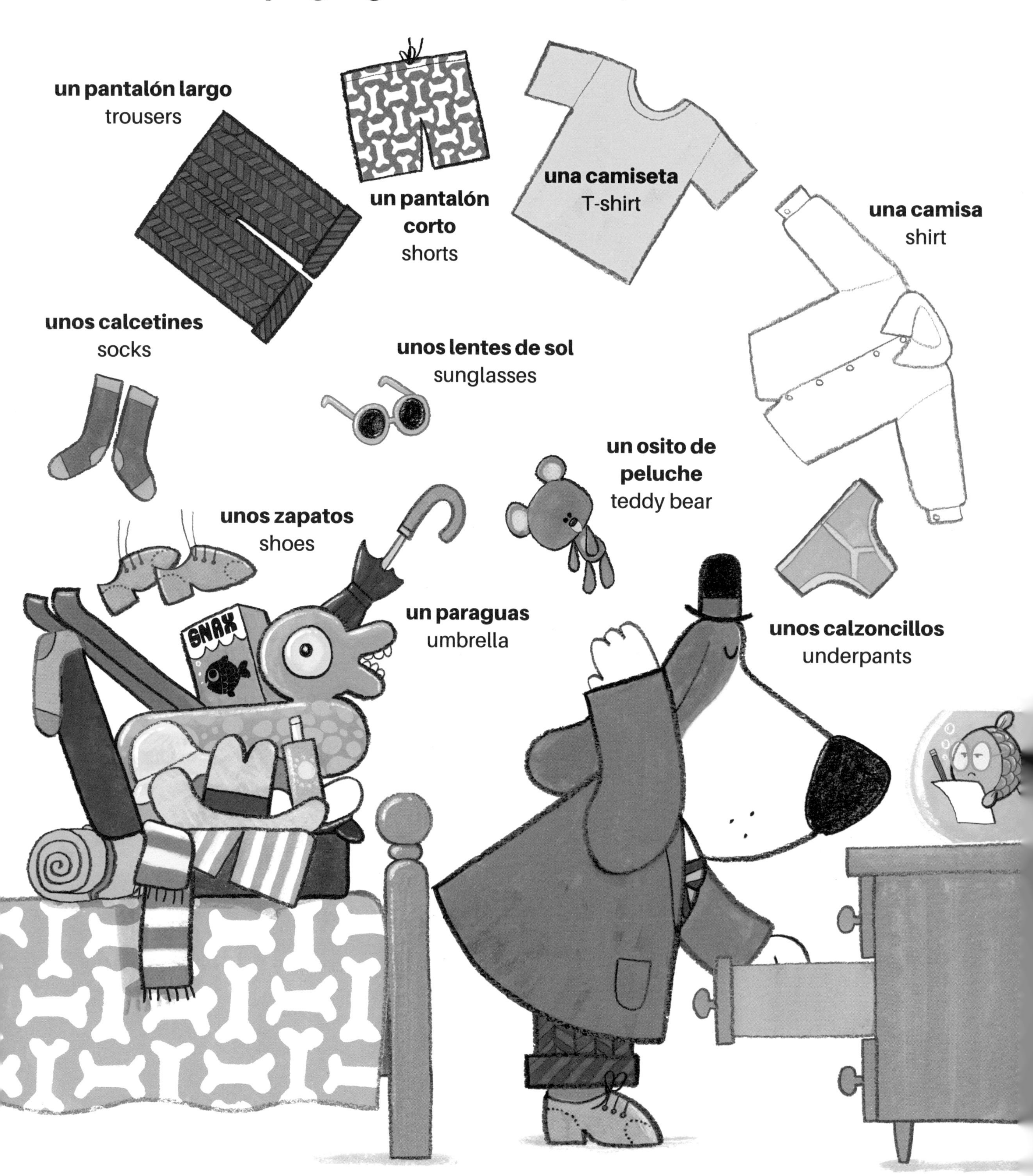

At last, señor Roscoe and Fry are ready to leave.

Have fun, señor Roscoe!

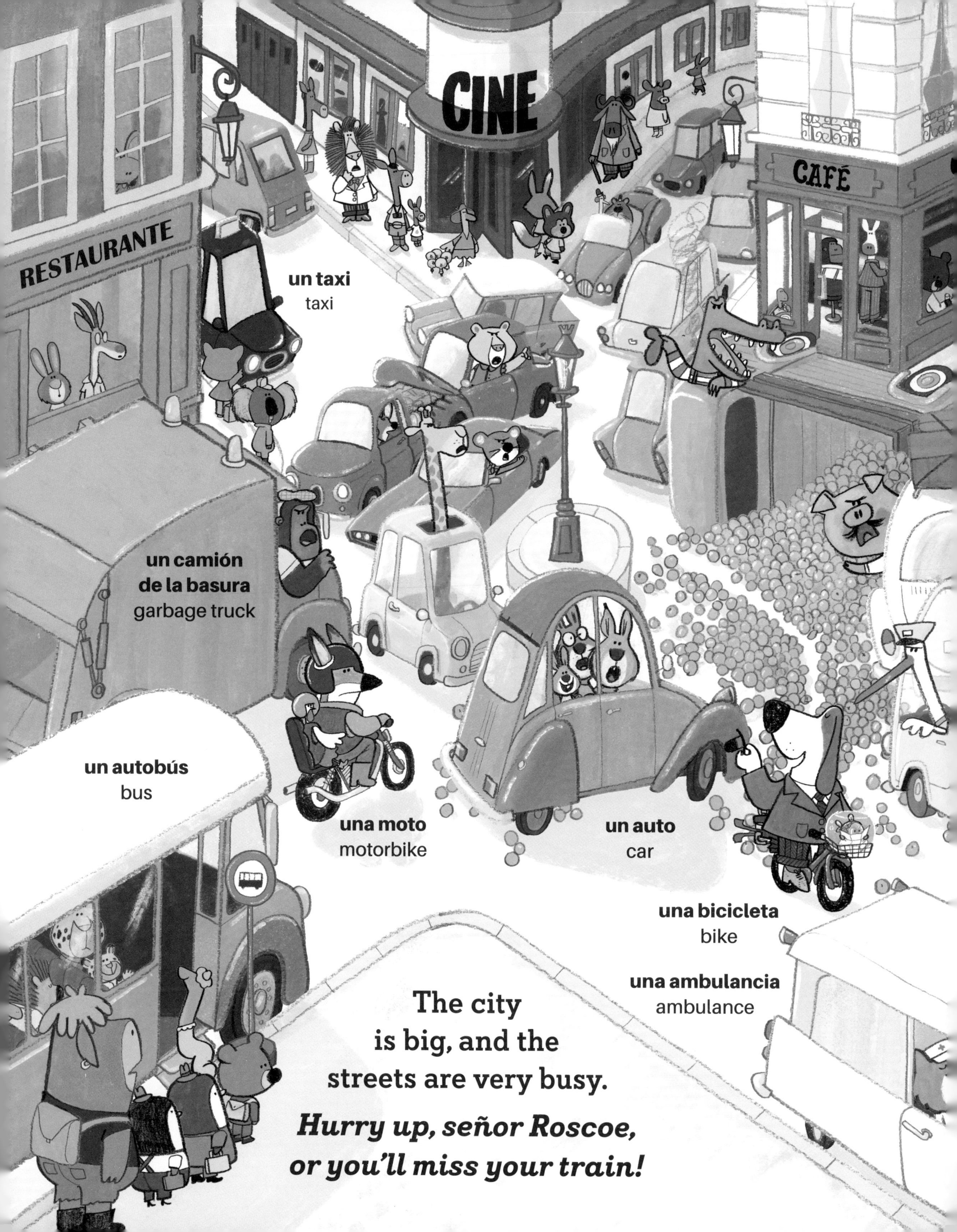

The city
is big, and the
streets are very busy.

***Hurry up, señor Roscoe,
or you'll miss your train!***

TIENDA DE COMESTIBLES
PELUQUERÍA
PANADERÍA
PANADERÍA
PASTELES
ABIERTO
n camión
e correos
nail truck
un escúter
scooter
un auto de policía
police car

Señor Roscoe and Fry catch the train, just in time.

Phew! That was close!

The train goes into the tunnel . . .

. . . and comes out into the countryside.

Señor Roscoe and Fry are going camping with their friend Eva.
Oh no, it's starting to rain!
¡Está lloviendo! It's raining!
¡Venga, rápido! Come quickly!

Señor Roscoe has brought his camping gear, but – oh dear! – he doesn't know how to put up a tent.

Luckily, Eva can help.

Where's your teddy, señor Roscoe?

After a night under the stars, it's time to say *adiós.*

Soon señor Roscoe and Fry are on a bus, traveling up into the snowy mountains.

They catch a lift to the very top of the ski slopes.

Señor Roscoe is looking
for his friend Stan.
¡Ya voy!
I'm coming!
¡Buenos días,
Stan!
Hello, Stan!
There he is,
skiing down the mountain.
Hang on tight, señor Roscoe!

It’s a long way down from the top of the mountain . . .

Oh crumbs, señor Roscoe, that’s the ski jump!

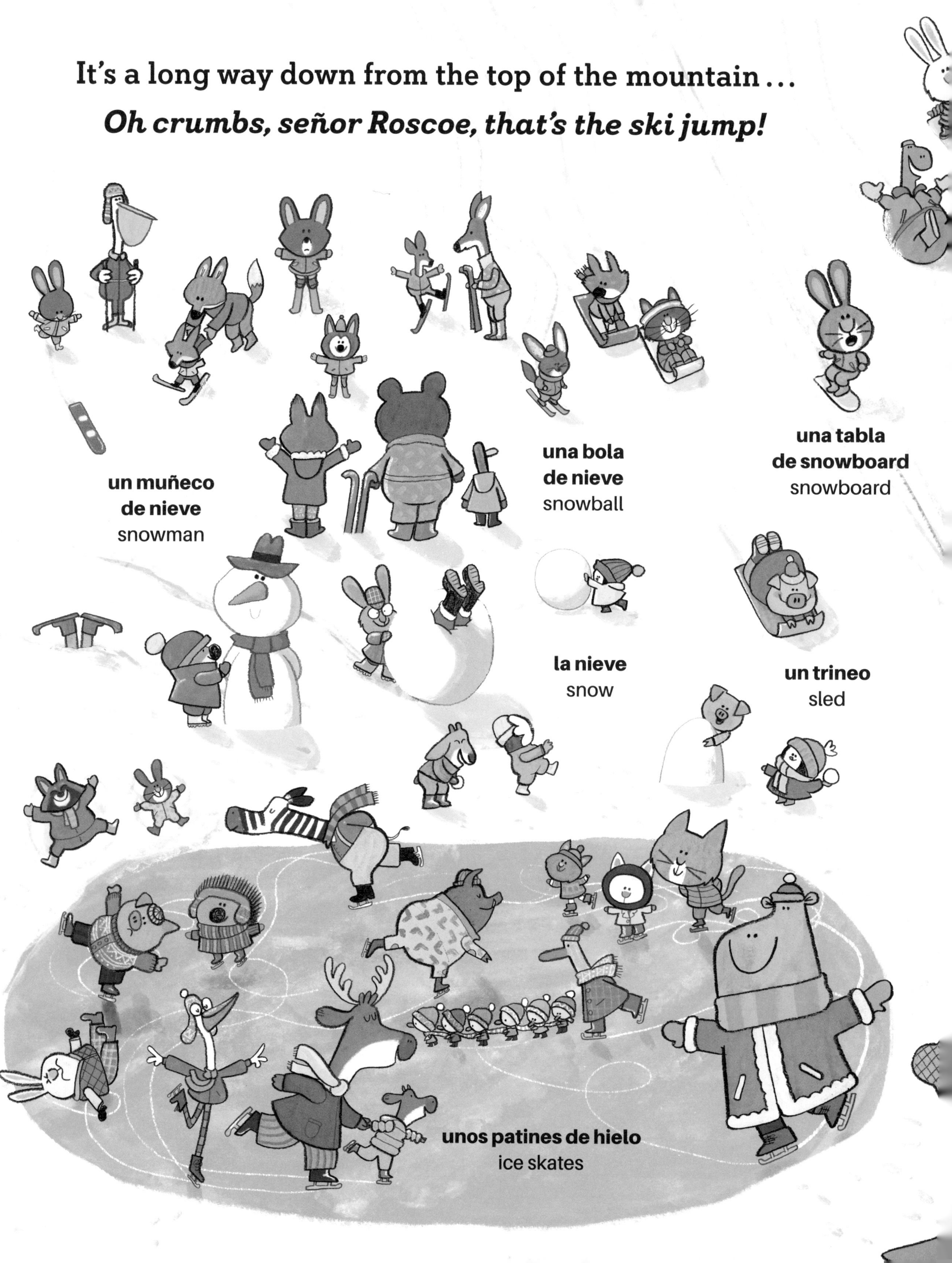

Wowee!

Stan and the crowd are very impressed!

Stan would like to take señor Roscoe snowboarding. But it's time to move on. ***Next time, señor Roscoe.***

It's hard work cycling to the lake.

Time for a rest, señor Roscoe?

Señor Roscoe and Fry are glad to see their friend Caro. She is going to take them for a trip on her boat!
¡Hola, Caro!
Hi, Caro!
¡Ahí está!
There you are!

el bosque
forest
una colina
hill
un velero
sailboat
una casa flotante
houseboat
un bote de pesca
fishing boat
una barca de remos
rowboat
una canoa
canoe
el lago
lake
una tabla de paddle
paddleboard
una balsa
raft

Señor Roscoe wants to try steering the boat. But it isn't as easy as it looks . . .

Watch out, señor Roscoe!

All too soon, it's time to go. Caro helps them find a big boat to take them on their way . . .

The next stop is señor Roscoe's favorite place . . .

. . . the seaside!

Señor Roscoe can’t wait to go swimming
with his friends Jojo and Didi.

Señor Roscoe loves splashing in the sea.
Everyone is very impressed with his floaty!
un salvavidas
lifeguard
una cometa
kite
un traje de baño
swimsuit
una toalla
towel
una sombrilla
umbrella
la playa
beach
la crema
solar
sunscreen
un castillo de arena
sandcastle

la natación
swimming
el surf
surfing
el mar
sea
las olas
waves
un flotador
floaty
unas raquetas
racquets

Señor Roscoe and Fry have had a wonderful time at the beach, but there is still one more friend to visit.

They take a taxi to a pretty little village.

Look where you're going, señor Roscoe!

Is that your tummy rumbling, señor Roscoe?
Maybe their old friend Dougal knows a good café.
Tengo hambre.
I'm hungry.
Yo también.
Me too.

Señor Roscoe and Dougal order TWO ice creams each, and a big fruity drink for Fry.
el pan
bread
el agua
water
un café
coffee
una ensalada
salad
un jugo
juice
un helado
ice cream

una hamburguesa
burger
unas aceitunas
olives
el queso
cheese
una silla
chair
un pastel
cake
unas
papas fritas
French fries
una mesa
table
Menú
unos plátanos
bananas
This is the life, señor Roscoe!

What a wonderful trip! But now, it's time to go home.

Señor Roscoe and Fry have had great fun with all of their friends.

Don't worry, señor Roscoe, you'll see them again soon.

After a long journey, señor Roscoe and Fry make it back home to the city.

Señor Roscoe has had a fantastic vacation.
But it's good to be back home.

Buenas noches, señor Roscoe.

Buenas noches, Fry.

Buenas noches, **everybody.**

Buenas noches.
Good night.

Señor Roscoe and Fry hope you've had fun with them on vacation. Can you spot the following items in the book?

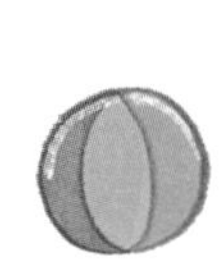

IN THE CITY

- **orange car**
  un auto anaranjado
- **hairdresser**
  un peluquero
- **pigeon**
  una paloma

ON THE SLOPES

- **tiger**
  un tigre
- **6 yellow ducklings**
  6 patitos amarillos
- **zebra**
  una cebra

AT THE SEASIDE

- **beach ball**
  una pelota de playa
- **surfer**
  un surfista
- **6 crabs**
  6 cangrejos

ON THE CAMPSITE

- **pink tent**
  una tienda de campaña rosada
- **guitar**
  una guitarra
- **bird**
  un pájaro

ON THE LAKE

- **2 fishermen**
  2 pescadores
- **4 fish**
  4 peces
- **mouse**
  un ratón

AT THE CAFÉ

- **baby leopard**
  un bebé leopardo
- **pizza**
  una pizza
- **hen**
  una gallina

First American Edition 2020
Kane Miller, A Division of EDC Publishing

First published in Great Britain in 2020 by Hodder and Stoughton,
an imprint of Hachette Children's Group, An Hachette UK Company.

 For information contact:
Kane Miller, A Division of EDC Publishing
www.kanemiller.com
www.usbornebooksandmore.com
Library of Congress Control Number: 2019957537
10 9 8 7 6 5 4 3 2
Printed and bound in China
ISBN: 978-1-68464-181-9

To "mon amour" Sandy. Thanks to your ideas, patience, support, encouragement and French! Without you, this book would never have existed. Merci beaucoup ma chérie!